Can I Have Some Cake Too?

A Story about Food Allergies and Friendship

by Melanie Nazareth

Illustrated by Shirley Lehner-Rhoades

Inspired by Andrew and Michelle Nazareth

www.hopeforallergies.org

This is a work of fiction. All names, characters, places, and incidents are either products of the author's imagination or used fictitiously. No reference to any real person is intended or should be inferred. Likeness of any situations to any persons living or dead is purely coincidental.

Book design by River Sanctuary Graphic Arts

The illustrations in this book were rendered in watercolors.

ISBN 978-1-935914-28-0

Library of Congress Control Number: 2013946192

Printed in the United States of America

Additional copies available from:

www.hopeforallergies.org

RIVER SANCTUARY PUBLISHING
P.O. Box 1561
Felton, CA 95018
www.riversanctuarypublishing.com
Dedicated to the awakening of the New Earth

Acknowledgments

Many thanks to David Weiss, Annie Elizabeth Porter, Shirley Lehner-Rhoades, Dr. Kari Nadeau, Dr. Daniel Kim, Steve Sweeney, Vidya Kilambi, Dr. Philippe Bégin, Tina Dominguez, Brian Hom, Chris Surowiec, Kimberley Yates Grosso, Leslie Adato, my husband Kevin and children Andrew and Michelle for their inspiration, enthusiasm and continued support.

For my parents, the late Basil Coutinho and Coryl Coutinho
whose lives brim with hope and a desire to make a difference

Foreword

Melanie Nazareth's *Can I Have Some Cake Too?* is a wonderful book for all ages, for adults and children alike. It is written for a broad audience, including those with and without food allergies. The format is excellent and helps answer questions with clear, informed explanations. It is a "must read" for teachers, students, principals, parents, and health professionals and I hope it is used as a teaching tool for many schools and clinics. Melanie Nazareth as an author understands the different issues involved in food allergy and her words will have broad impact in the field of food allergy to help others.

Kari Nadeau, MD, PhD, FAAAAI
Stanford University School of Medicine
Lucile Packard Children's Hospital
Stanford Hospital and Clinics
Division of Allergy, Immunology, and Rheumatology
Nadissy Family Foundation Associate Professor
Director, Stanford Alliance for Food Allergy Research (SAFAR)

My heart leapt with joy when I saw a beautiful cake with candles, on the art table, after dropoff at school.

Whose birthday is it today? I wondered. *Will the cake have nuts? Can I eat it?*

YUMMM...DELICIOUS...I LOVE BIRTHDAY CAKE!!

I ran off to play with my friends on the playground. Our playground has beautiful beds of vibrant, colorful flowers, a nice patch of green grass and a sturdy red play structure that we love playing on.

“Hey Michelle,” said Troy as he glided down the slide. “Today is Julia’s birthday!”

“Where is she?” I asked as I gleefully followed Troy.

Just then we saw Julia, who looked radiant in her pretty pink dress. She floated towards us like an elegant swan.

“Hi Troy! Hi Michelle!” Julia said with a broad grin on her face.

“Happy birthday, Julia!” Troy and I said as we gave her a big hug.

“Hey...did you see my birthday cake?” Julia asked excitedly.

“Yup…it looks DELICIOUS. I love the pink roses on it,” I said as I admired the cake with longing eyes.

“Look! It has blue roses on it too!!” exclaimed Troy.

“Pink and blue are my favorite colors! My mom sat up all night decorating it,” said Julia proudly.

Does it have nuts? I pondered again. I'm allergic to peanuts and some tree nuts. My mom told me that I should NEVER eat birthday cake unless she confirms to me that it has NO PEANUTS AND NO TREE NUTS.

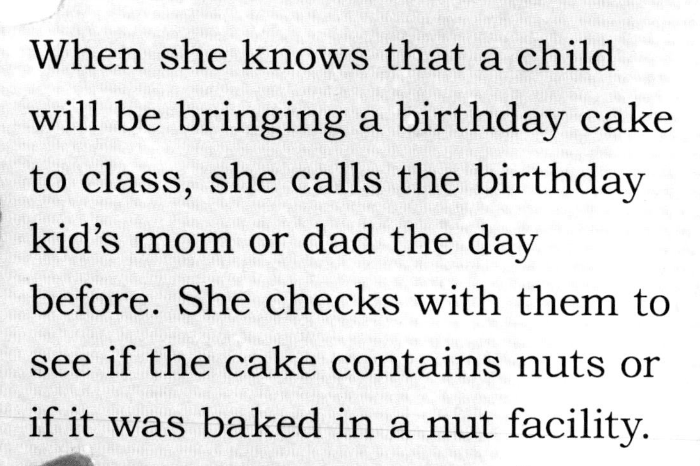

When she knows that a child will be bringing a birthday cake to class, she calls the birthday kid's mom or dad the day before. She checks with them to see if the cake contains nuts or if it was baked in a nut facility. Then she gives me the go-ahead to eat the cake.

"Does it have nuts?" I asked Julia nervously as we picked flowers for the vase in our classroom.

"I don't know...Oh, it looks so pretty, I'm sure a small piece won't hurt you," said Julia with a reassuring smile.

"Ummm...I'm not sure I can have a slice of your birthday cake today," I whispered to Julia.

I felt disappointed and sad.

My mouth began to water.

I LOVE BIRTHDAY CAKE!!! I HOPE JULIA'S CAKE HAS NO NUTS...

Just then the school bell rang. Mrs. Robinson asked us to line up for class. I couldn't stop thinking of the cake. *Pink roses... blue roses*. Today we will learn about the planets during circle time. But all I could think of was Julia's birthday cake perched prettily on the table.

"Jupiter, Mars, Venus, Saturn..." We began naming the planets. Suddenly the planets that were hanging from the ceiling looked like little birthday cakes to me. They had different colors. Red, yellow, blue, green, brown, grey...all with pink and blue roses...they looked DELICIOUS.

Do THEY have nuts?? I asked myself.

"What are you thinking about?" asked Julia quietly.

"Your delicious birthday cake, Julia," I replied, surprised.

"I'm sure you can have a small bite," Julia whispered. "I bet just one tiny piece won't make you sick. It's my birthday cake. It's special!"

"Maybe," I said a little hesitantly. The planets swirled around me as I heard Mrs. Robinson's voice in the background. *What was their flavor? Chocolate? Vanilla?*

All I could think of was cake. I truly wanted to taste Julia's cake...even if it was just a tiny piece.

I don't want to have an allergy. Maybe I'll get hives. I"ll begin to choke. Maybe Mrs. Robinson will have to give me epinephrine... she will have to call 911...I'll have to go to the emergency room. I can even die from it, my thoughts raced.

“This is sooooo not fair,” I complained to Troy during our free time.

Why me?? I thought to myself. *Maybe I could take a chance just this once.*

Then I remembered my mom’s instructions to wait for her approval before eating food served at school.

"Oh, c'mon Michelle. You know you shouldn't do that," said Troy with worry on his face. "You know getting an allergic reaction is not good for you," he continued solemnly. "I have an idea...I won't have Julia's cake either. Instead we'll have the nut-free treats your mom keeps with Mrs. Robinson," said Troy sympathetically.

"That's kind of you Troy, you're a good friend to support me," I replied gratefully. "But, I want to try it anyway. I LOVE BIRTHDAY CAKE. I really want a piece today," I said stubbornly, knowing that I wasn't making a good decision.

Vanilla cake with red and blue roses...

You see, birthdays are a big deal at school. Our moms and dads bring in a cake for us. After circle time, we all gather around the birthday child, and make a wish for him or her.

We sing... "Happy Birthday to you...cha...cha...cha..." and then... the boy or girl makes a wish...blows the candles out...*whoosh*! and then......WE EAT THE BIRTHDAY CAKE. YUMMM!! DELICIOUS!!

And now it was time to eat Julia's birthday cake. I was so excited!

Soon, I began to get nervous. Troy and I decided not to eat the cake. I knew I had to wait for my mom's approval to eat *any* birthday cake.

Maybe she forgot to ask Julia's mom. Maybe she asked her but forgot to tell me. Well, I'll ask Mrs. Robinson to call my mom and ask her for permission! I thought, determined to take care of myself. I wanted Troy to be able to enjoy the cake too.

"Mrs. Robinson, I really want to eat Julia's cake," I said. "Please can you call my mom and ask her if she checked that Julia's cake is nut free?" I asked softly.

"Of course, Michelle," agreed Mrs. Robinson, who went to her office to call my mom.
I waited anxiously. *Why me?*
I pitied myself again.

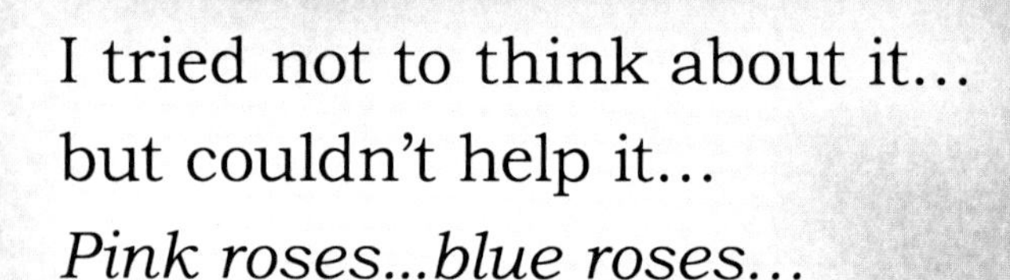

I tried not to think about it...
but couldn't help it...
Pink roses...blue roses...

Mrs. Robinson came out smiling. She said that my mom forgot to tell me this morning that she checked with Julia's mom last night.

The cake *is* nut free, and safe for me to eat.

YES!!! I can have the cake.

YES!!! I can taste the pink roses.

Yes!!! I can savor – not just a tiny sliver – but a whole slice!

YUMMM!!..........DELICIOUS!!!

YIPPEE!!! I was thrilled.

I am so glad I didn't take the risk and make a bad decision. I am so glad that Troy is such a good friend and showed me his support. I am so glad I asked Mrs. Robinson to call my mom.

I was SOOOO EXCITED. I COULD HAVE SOME BIRTHDAY CAKE, TOO!!

PINK ROSES...BLUE ROSES…

I LOVE BIRTHDAY CAKE!

Happy Birthday to you, Julia...cha...cha...cha...

In memory of BJ Hom, Natalie Giorgi and all those who tragically lost their lives due to food allergies.

Helpful Food Allergy Websites

For more information on food allergy risks to children, refer to the following websites:

FARE – Food Allergy Research & Education
www.foodallergy.org/

The American Academy of Allergy, Asthma and Immunology
www.aaaai.org/

Kids With Food Allergies
www.kidswithfoodallergies.org/

MedHelp
http://www.medhelp.org/allergies

Consortium of Food Allergy Research (CoFAR)
http://www.cofargroup.org/

Best Allergy Sites: Allergy Information Guide
www.bestallergysites.com/

Opportunities for Discussion

1. What was Michelle's reaction when she first saw Julia's birthday cake in school?
2. What were Michelle's concerns about eating the birthday cake?
3. Which friend in the book – Julia or Troy - was more supportive of Michelle while she struggled about her dilemma to eat the birthday cake?
4. In what way did Troy help Michelle to be cautious?
5. Do you have a food allergy? What would you do in Michelle's place?
6. If you don't have a food allergy, how would you support a friend who has one?
7. How did Michelle help herself to be safe from getting a food allergy attack, by doing the right thing?
8. How did Michelle's teacher help her?
9. If you are not sure if a birthday cake or a food contains allergens that you are allergic to, what would you do to protect yourself from getting a food allergy attack?
10. What was Michelle's reaction when she knew that she could have some cake too?

About the Author

Melanie Nazareth holds Master's degrees in English and in Television, Radio and Film. Her career includes writing and producing documentaries on the World Bank and UN family, TV syndication and business development. Her daily experiences with keeping both of her children with food allergies safe and helping them navigate their challenges at school and social gatherings inspired her to write *Can I Have Some Cake Too?* She is actively involved as a food allergy advocate in the San Francisco Bay Area. Melanie lives with her family in California.

For more information visit: *www.hopeforallergies.org*

About the Artist

Shirley Lehner-Rhoades is a fine art painter and an art instructor to kids and adults in the Santa Cruz area. She loves living near the ocean where she finds many inspiring backdrops for her paintings.

CPSIA information can be obtained
at www.ICGtesting.com
Printed in the USA
BVXC01n0952050216
435315BV00006B/26

* 9 7 8 1 9 3 5 9 1 4 2 8 0 *